MIDNIGHT -

DEBRAJ SAHA

Made with ♥ on the Notion Press Platform
www.notionpress.com

Contents

I

Ding dong! The bell rang, Leo opened the door, there was no one behind the door. He closed it and turned and again the bell rang, ding dong! Who is doing this nonsense with me at midnight?

"Who's there?" he asked loudly. No answer came back to him. "What the hell are you playing, who keeps ringing my bell like a madman?" Leo muttered angrily and went to the bedroom. There were two windows in his room, both of which had been open for quite some time. Maybe that's how someone got into the house? He sat down on the bed and turned the light off. After a few minutes he heard steps coming from the hallway towards his room, but they didn't stop when they reached his door. They continued further into the house. It sounded as if somebody was searching through the whole house: clattering of feet, and then the noise stopped right outside his bedroom window. Leo listened carefully and saw movement near the window, but he couldn't make out what it was; the moonlight wasn't enough to reveal anything. But whatever it was, it looked like a young man. Some one whispered on Leo's ear "Ha ha ha get out of this room" and everything around him went black. A hand grabbed his throat and lifted him up off the floor. Then he felt himself being carried away. He tried to fight against it, but his hands were tied and he couldn't move them. The next moment he felt something heavy hit his head. And then darkness.

The next morning, Leo woke up in pain. His neck hurt so much that he could hardly breathe. He tried to sit up, but his head started spinning and he fell back onto the pillow. He looked around and saw his friend was sitting beside him. He smiled at him and said "you're awake.", Leo slowly got out of bed. He began to feel dizzy immediately. His legs gave way under him. He caught hold of him and supported him.

"You have a terrible headache," he said. "Sit down, I'll get you some water." Leo couldn't believe what was going on. "Why did you bring me here?" he asked. "I'm not sure what's happening to you", he added. "Where am I? What happened to me last night? You know, we should go to the doctor."

His friend didn't reply. He just sat there quietly looking at him. The boy stood up and left the room. Leo collapsed onto the bed and stayed there until his friend returned with some warm water. He drank it all without even tasting it. Then he lay down on the bed and slept. When he woke up he felt better. His friend was still asleep, so he decided to start exploring the place. It was the time of evening, he was exploring the place suddenly some one touched his shoulder, he quickly looked back and saw it was his friend Nick. "Oh it's you don't give me jump scares", said Leo.

"Look what I found", said Nick pointing to a mirror. "What do you think about this?", he asked. He walked into the bathroom and switched on the lights. A young man appeared in the mirror. He wore a dark blue suit and had a long curly brown hair. He looked exactly like Leo, except for his eyes. His eyes were completely black. "I don't understand what's happening, why am I seeing myself?" he asked. "This doesn't make any sense!", he screamed. "This isn't possible!"

He ran out of the bathroom and looked around. In the kitchen he saw a tray lying on the table. On it was an egg with a spider crawling inside it. He picked up the tray and threw it across the room. "What is this?", he yelled.

Nick woke up from where he was standing and looked at the wall. "It looks like there's some kind of mirror over there", he said. "Let's go check it out". They went to the other side of the mirror and looked at themselves. They were surprised to see that they weren't there.

"There's nothing here", said Leo. "We must be hallucinating or something like that. Let's forget about it."

They went back to their room and laid down on the bed. It was getting late and they both wanted to sleep. They were tired after the crazy day. Suddenly, Leo felt somebody touch his arm. He looked up and saw the reflection of him in the mirror. Someone whispered on Leo's ear "You will die".

Leo got scared. He jumped off the bed and tried to run out of the room, but he was pulled back by his friend.

"What's the matter?", asked Nick. "Are you alright?"

"No, I'm not okay. Look what's happening to me", he said. "Somebody is messing with my head. This isn't real."

"Calm down Leo, I'll call the police", said Nick. Leo shook his head. "You can't do that, I'm not imagining this", he said. "I've seen this face in the mirror, and now you're saying this isn't real?"

Leo looked in the mirror again. He saw his friend Nick standing behind him. "Wait, I want to show you something", said Leo. "When I look in the mirror I see you too".

"I told you it's not real, but you won't listen to me", said Nick. They argued for a while, and then Leo decided to take a shower. He took a deep breath and stepped into the bathroom. The moment he entered the bathroom he heard the sound of somebody knocking on the door. "Who's there?", he asked. Silence. He shut the door and turned the water on. The second he turned the water on he felt something scratch his back. He turned around and screamed. Standing in front of him was a tall man wearing a black leather jacket. His face was covered with bandages. "You're dead", he shouted. He pushed Leo against the wall and held him tight. "I can't believe you're alive", he said.

Then the man disappeared and everything went black.

***

"I don't know how many times I have to tell you to stay away from me. Why do you keep following me and trying to kill me?" asked Leo.

"Because you're mine", said the voice. "Leave this place before I kill you."

"I'm not yours", shouted Leo. "You're not real".

He heard footsteps approaching and a loud thud. Then everything went black.

Leo woke up with a sharp pain in his head. He felt as if he was punched in the face. He was lying on the floor. He got up and noticed that his head was bleeding. He was dizzy and nauseous. He got up and stumbled to the bathroom. He felt weak and couldn't stand. He tried to find his bearings but he couldn't focus his eyes. He fell on the bathroom floor.

He looked around and saw his friend Nick standing in front of him. "Good morning", he said.

"Get out of my way!", Leo shouted. "I'm sick and tired of your bullshit."

"I need you to talk to me", said Nick. "Do it or I'll kill you."

Leo struggled to get up and ran into the kitchen. He grabbed some water and brought it to his mouth and began drinking. He drank a lot of water and then sat down on the chair. He looked at his friend. He looked like he was in his early twenties. His skin was pale and he had a short brown hair. "You're not really here, right?" asked Leo.

"Yes, I'm real", said Nick. "And I'm not going anywhere."

"How do you know my name?" asked Leo. "Why are you here?"

"You have to be honest with yourself", said Nick. "Don't you remember me?"

Leo shook his head. "I don't know you", he replied. "I never met you before."

"That's because you're lying", said Nick. "You know me very well indeed. You've seen me in the mirror."

"I'm sorry, but this is just a dream", said Leo. "I'm not going to harm you, if that's what you're afraid of."

"You're lying again!", said Nick. "You'll die tonight."

"Stop making this up", said Leo.

Nick laughed. "But I am real, aren't I?" he asked.

"Please leave me alone", pleaded Leo. "Just go away".

"No way", said Nick. "I want to know how you're going to die."

"Listen to me", said Leo. "I don't know what you're talking about. Just leave me alone."

"You don't know how to end your life, do you?" asked Nick. "Or maybe you want to kill people? If you commit suicide you might as well kill someone else instead."

Leo couldn't believe what he was hearing. He stared at his friend in disbelief. "This is insane", he exclaimed. "I'm not going to kill anyone".

"Who do you love?" asked Nick. "Come on, give it up. Tell me who you love."

"I don't love anybody", said Leo. "I only care about myself."

"Even though you're dying?" asked Nick. "You don't even love yourself?"

"I only care about myself", said Leo. "I'll let you go when you promise to leave me alone."

"I'm not leaving you alone ever again", said Nick. "You're going to die tonight."

"I'm not going to do anything", said Leo. "Just let me go."

"I can see your soul", said Nick. "You're lying to yourself. You're always thinking about someone else. Everyone wants something from you. That's why you're going to die tonight."

"I'm not going to do anything", said Leo. "I don't know what you're talking about. Please leave me alone."

"You'll die tonight, and I will be watching", said Nick.

Leo woke up screaming. He saw his friend standing above him. "I'll take you to the hospital", said Nick. "What happened to you?"

"I saw a ghost", said Leo. "I thought I was going crazy, but I guess I wasn't."

"Did you tell anyone?" asked Nick.

"No", said Leo. "I didn't want them to worry about me."

"They would've been more concerned if they knew what was happening to you", said Nick. "I don't know why you didn't tell them anything."

"I didn't want to bother anyone", said Leo. "I figured it was just a nightmare."

"Well, it's no longer a nightmare", said Nick. "I'm not leaving you alone anymore."

"Why are you doing this to me?", asked Leo. "Is this some kind of joke?"

"Everything is serious to me", said Nick. "Now come with me."

Leo got dressed and followed his friend outside. They walked through the streets until they reached a big house. Leo remembered that he had seen this place once before. He didn't know why but he felt uneasy.

"I have to go inside", said Leo. "I don't feel safe outside."

"Be careful", said Nick. "You should stay close to me."

They went into the house and Leo could see the whole thing had been renovated. There were new windows and walls everywhere. "Have you done all of this by yourself?", asked Leo.

"Yes", said Nick. "This is my house, and I'm going to live here from now on."

Leo looked around the living room. Everything was clean except for one corner of the room. The floor was covered with dust and there was a huge pile of junk.

"What's that?", asked Leo.

"That's where you'll die", said Nick.

Leo looked at his friend's face. It was covered in bandages. "What do you mean?", he asked. "How did you get hurt?"

"Remember when you told me not to follow you?", asked Nick. "That day you got into an accident."

"I remember", said Leo. "What about it?"

"If you hadn't told me to stay away, I wouldn't have followed you", said Nick. "I wouldn't have gotten hurt."

"So you blame me for getting injured", said Leo. "Is that what you're telling me?"

"I don't know what happened that day", said Nick. "But I know you caused it."

Scary Night Experience.

Make this story more longer:

Ding dong! The bell rang, Leo opened the door, there was no one behind the door. He closed it and turned and again the bell rang, ding dong! Who is doing this nonsense with me at midnight?

"Who's there?" he asked loudly. No answer came back to him. "What the hell are you playing, who keeps ringing my bell like a madman?" Leo muttered angrily and went to the bedroom. There were two windows in his room, both of which had been open for quite some time. Maybe that's how someone got into the house? He sat down on the bed and turned the light off. After a few minutes he heard steps coming from the hallway towards his room, but they didn't stop when they reached his door. They continued further into the house. It sounded as if somebody was searching through the whole house: clattering of feet, and then the noise stopped right outside his bedroom window. Leo listened carefully and saw movement near the window, but he couldn't make out what it was; the moonlight wasn't enough to reveal anything. But whatever it was, it looked like a young man. Some one whispered on Leo's ear "Ha ha ha get out of this room" and everything around him went black. A hand grabbed his throat and lifted him up off the floor. Then he felt himself being carried away. He tried to fight against it, but his hands were tied and he couldn't move them. The next moment he felt something heavy hit his head. And then darkness.

The next morning, Leo woke up in pain. His neck hurt so much that he could hardly breathe. He tried to sit up, but his head started spinning and he fell back onto the pillow. He looked around and saw his friend was sitting beside him. He smiled at him and said "you're awake.", Leo slowly got out of bed. He began to feel dizzy immediately. His legs gave way under him. He caught hold of him and supported him.

"You have a terrible headache," he said. "Sit down, I'll get you some water." Leo couldn't believe what was going on. "Why did you bring me here?" he asked. "I'm not sure what's happening to you", he added. "Where am I? What happened to me last night? You know, we should go to the doctor."

His friend didn't reply. He just sat there quietly looking at him. The boy stood up and left the room. Leo collapsed onto the bed and stayed there until his friend returned with some warm water. He drank it all without even tasting it. Then he lay down on the bed and slept. When he woke up he felt better. His friend was still asleep, so he decided to start exploring the place. It was the time of evening, he was exploring the place suddenly some one touched his shoulder, he quickly looked back and saw it was his friend Nick. "Oh it's you don't give me jump scares", said Leo.

"Look what I found", said Nick pointing to a mirror. "What do you think about this?", he asked. He walked into the bathroom and switched on the lights. A young man appeared in the mirror. He wore a dark blue suit and had a long curly brown hair. He looked exactly like Leo, except for his eyes. His eyes were completely black. "I don't understand what's happening, why am I seeing myself?" he asked. "This doesn't make any sense!", he screamed. "This isn't possible!"

He ran out of the bathroom and looked around. In the kitchen he saw a tray lying on the table. On it was an egg with a spider crawling inside it. He picked up the tray and threw it across the room. "What is this?", he yelled.

Nick woke up from where he was standing and looked at the wall. "It looks like there's some kind of mirror over there", he said. "Let's go check it out". They went to the other side of the mirror and looked at themselves. They were surprised to see that they weren't there.

"There's nothing here", said Leo. "We must be hallucinating or something like that. Let's forget about it."

They went back to their room and laid down on the bed. It was getting late and they both wanted to sleep. They were tired after the crazy day. Suddenly, Leo felt somebody touch his arm. He looked up and saw the reflection of him in the mirror. Someone whispered on Leo's ear "You will die".

Leo got scared. He jumped off the bed and tried to run out of the room, but he was pulled back by his friend.

"What's the matter?", asked Nick. "Are you alright?"

"No, I'm not okay. Look what's happening to me", he said. "Somebody is messing with my head. This isn't real."

"Calm down Leo, I'll call the police", said Nick. Leo shook his head. "You can't do that, I'm not imagining this", he said. "I've seen this face in the mirror, and now you're saying this isn't real?"

Leo looked in the mirror again. He saw his friend Nick standing behind him. "Wait, I want to show you something", said Leo. "When I look in the mirror I see you too".

"I told you it's not real, but you won't listen to me", said Nick. They argued for a while, and then Leo decided to take a shower. He took a deep breath and stepped into the bathroom. The moment he entered the bathroom he heard the sound of somebody knocking on the door. "Who's there?", he asked. Silence. He shut the door and turned the water on. The second he turned the water on he felt something scratch his back. He turned around and screamed. Standing in front of him was a tall man wearing a black leather jacket. His face was covered with bandages. "You're dead", he shouted. He pushed Leo against the wall and held him tight. "I can't believe you're alive", he said.

Then the man disappeared and everything went black.

***

"I don't know how many times I have to tell you to stay away from me. Why do you keep following me and trying to kill me?" asked Leo.

"Because you're mine", said the voice. "Leave this place before I kill you."

"I'm not yours", shouted Leo. "You're not real".

He heard footsteps approaching and a loud thud. Then everything went black.

Leo woke up with a sharp pain in his head. He felt as if he was punched in the face. He was lying on the floor. He got up and noticed that his head was bleeding. He was dizzy and nauseous. He got up and stumbled to the bathroom. He felt weak and couldn't stand. He tried to find his bearings but he couldn't focus his eyes. He fell on the bathroom floor.

He looked around and saw his friend Nick standing in front of him. "Good morning", he said.

"Get out of my way!", Leo shouted. "I'm sick and tired of your bullshit."

"I need you to talk to me", said Nick. "Do it or I'll kill you."

Leo struggled to get up and ran into the kitchen. He grabbed some water and brought it to his mouth and began drinking. He drank a lot of water and then sat down on the chair. He looked at his friend. He looked like he was in his early twenties. His skin was pale and he had a short brown hair. "You're not really here, right?" asked Leo.

"Yes, I'm real", said Nick. "And I'm not going anywhere."

"How do you know my name?" asked Leo. "Why are you here?"

"You have to be honest with yourself", said Nick. "Don't you remember me?"

Leo shook his head. "I don't know you", he replied. "I never met you before."

"That's because you're lying", said Nick. "You know me very well indeed. You've seen me in the mirror."

"I'm sorry, but this is just a dream", said Leo. "I'm not going to harm you, if that's what you're afraid of."

"You're lying again!", said Nick. "You'll die tonight."

"Stop making this up", said Leo.

Nick laughed. "But I am real, aren't I?" he asked.

"Please leave me alone", pleaded Leo. "Just go away".

"No way", said Nick. "I want to know how you're going to die."

"Listen to me", said Leo. "I don't know what you're talking about. Just leave me alone."

"You don't know how to end your life, do you?" asked Nick. "Or maybe you want to kill people? If you commit suicide you might as well kill someone else instead."

Leo couldn't believe what he was hearing. He stared at his friend in disbelief. "This is insane", he exclaimed. "I'm not going to kill anyone".

"Who do you love?" asked Nick. "Come on, give it up. Tell me who you love."

"I don't love anybody", said Leo. "I only care about myself."

"Even though you're dying?" asked Nick. "You don't even love yourself?"

"I only care about myself", said Leo. "I'll let you go when you promise to leave me alone."

"I'm not leaving you alone ever again", said Nick. "You're going to die tonight."

"I'm not going to do anything", said Leo. "Just let me go."

"I can see your soul", said Nick. "You're lying to yourself. You're always thinking about someone else. Everyone wants something from you. That's why you're going to die tonight."

"I'm not going to do anything", said Leo. "I don't know what you're talking about. Please leave me alone."

"You'll die tonight, and I will be watching", said Nick.

Leo woke up screaming. He saw his friend standing above him. "I'll take you to the hospital", said Nick. "What happened to you?"

"I saw a ghost", said Leo. "I thought I was going crazy, but I guess I wasn't."

"Did you tell anyone?" asked Nick.

"No", said Leo. "I didn't want them to worry about me."

"They would've been more concerned if they knew what was happening to you", said Nick. "I don't know why you didn't tell them anything."

"I didn't want to bother anyone", said Leo. "I figured it was just a nightmare."

"Well, it's no longer a nightmare", said Nick. "I'm not leaving you alone anymore."

"Why are you doing this to me?", asked Leo. "Is this some kind of joke?"

"Everything is serious to me", said Nick. "Now come with me."

Leo got dressed and followed his friend outside. They walked through the streets until they reached a big house. Leo remembered that he had seen this place once before. He didn't know why but he felt uneasy.

"I have to go inside", said Leo. "I don't feel safe outside."

"Be careful", said Nick. "You should stay close to me."

They went into the house and Leo could see the whole thing had been renovated. There were new windows and walls everywhere. "Have you done all of this by yourself?", asked Leo.

"Yes", said Nick. "This is my house, and I'm going to live here from now on."

Leo looked around the living room. Everything was clean except for one corner of the room. The floor was covered with dust and there was a huge pile of junk.

"What's that?", asked Leo.

"That's where you'll die", said Nick.

Leo looked at his friend's face. It was covered in bandages. "What do you mean?", he asked. "How did you get hurt?"

"Remember when you told me not to follow you?", asked Nick. "That day you got into an accident."

"I remember", said Leo. "What about it?"

"If you hadn't told me to stay away, I wouldn't have followed you", said Nick. "I wouldn't have gotten hurt."

"So you blame me for getting injured", said Leo. "Is that what you're telling me?"

"I don't know what happened that day", said Nick. "But I know you caused it."

I'm sure it will pass.",said Leo

Leo jumped in pain and he quickly turned around to see what had scratched his back, but there was nothing there. He looked in the mirror, but the scratches weren't visible on his back. He was confused and scared at the same time. He finished taking his shower and went back to his room, where Nick was waiting for him.

"Did you hear that knocking on the door?" Leo asked Nick.

"No, I didn't hear anything," Nick replied.

"I also felt something scratch my back in the shower," Leo said, pointing to the scratches on his back.

Nick looked at the scratches, but he couldn't see anything.

"This is getting weirder by the minute," Nick said, looking around the room as if he expected something strange to happen.

Leo nodded in agreement, still feeling the sensation of the scratch on his back. He lay down on the bed and closed his eyes, trying to calm down. After a few minutes, he fell asleep.

He dreamed that he was in a forest, and someone was following him. He could hear footsteps behind him, but every time he turned around, there was no one there. Suddenly, he saw a figure standing in front of him, and it was the same young man he had seen near his window the night before. He had a sinister smile on his face.

"What do you want from me?" Leo asked.

"You know what I want," the young man said. "I want your soul."

Leo woke up screaming. Nick jumped up from the chair and rushed to Leo's side.

"Are you okay?" Nick asked, putting his hand on Leo's forehead.

"I had a nightmare," Leo said, still trembling.

Nick looked around the room, trying to find any signs of what could have caused Leo's nightmare, but everything seemed normal.

"We need to get out of here," Leo said, still feeling scared. "This place is not safe."

Nick nodded in agreement. They quickly packed their bags and left the room, not looking back.

As they were leaving the building, Leo noticed something strange. The building looked different from the outside. The windows were boarded up, and the door had a sign that read "condemned."

"What's going on?" Leo asked Nick.

"I don't know," Nick said, equally confused.

They walked a few blocks and finally found a police station. They went in and told the officers about their experience. The officers listened carefully and then asked them to describe the building.

After a few minutes of talking, the officers looked at each other and then turned to Leo and Nick.

"There's no such building in this area," one of the officers said. "Are you sure you're not making this up?"

"Did you hear that knocking on the door?" Leo asked Nick.

"No, I didn't hear anything," Nick replied.

"I also felt something scratch my back in the shower," Leo said, pointing to the scratches on his back.

Nick looked at the scratches, but he couldn't see anything.

"This is getting weirder by the minute," Nick said, looking around the room as if he expected something strange to happen.

Leo nodded in agreement, still feeling the sensation of the scratch on his back. He lay down on the bed and closed his eyes, trying to calm down. After a few minutes, he fell asleep.

He dreamed that he was in a forest, and someone was following him. He could hear footsteps behind him, but every time he turned around, there was no one there. Suddenly, he saw a figure standing in front of him, and it was the same young man he had seen near his window the night before. He had a sinister smile on his face.

"What do you want from me?" Leo asked.

"You know what I want," the young man said. "I want your soul."

Leo woke up screaming. Nick jumped up from the chair and rushed to Leo's side.

"Are you okay?" Nick asked, putting his hand on Leo's forehead.

"I had a nightmare," Leo said, still trembling.

Nick looked around the room, trying to find any signs of what could have caused Leo's nightmare, but everything seemed normal.

"We need to get out of here," Leo said, still feeling scared. "This place is not safe."

Nick nodded in agreement. They quickly packed their bags and left the room, not looking back.

As they were leaving the building, Leo noticed something strange. The building looked different from the outside. The windows were boarded up, and the door had a sign that read "condemned."

"What's going on?" Leo asked Nick.

"I don't know," Nick said, equally confused.

They walked a few blocks and finally found a police station. They went in and told the officers about their experience. The officers listened carefully and then asked them to describe the building.

After a few minutes of talking, the officers looked at each other and then turned to Leo and Nick.

"There's no such building in this area," one of the officers said. "Are you sure you're not making this up?"

Leo and Nick looked at each other in disbelief. They couldn't believe what they were hearing.

"We're not making this up," Leo said firmly. "We stayed in that building for the night. It was right there."

He pointed to the direction they had come from, but the officers only looked at each other and shook their heads.

"Sir, I'm sorry, but there's no such building here," the officer repeated.

Leo and Nick couldn't understand what was going on. They were sure they had stayed in that building, but now they were being told it didn't exist.

"Can you at least check the records?" Nick asked. "Maybe there was a building there at some point."

The officers nodded and went to check the records. After a few minutes, they came back and looked at Leo and Nick with a puzzled expression.

"You're right," one of the officers said. "There used to be a building there, but it was torn down over 10 years ago. No one has stayed there since then."

Leo and Nick couldn't believe what they were hearing. They had just spent the night in a building that didn't exist. They were both shaken and didn't know what to do next.

The officers offered to take them back to the area to show them that there was no building there, but Leo and Nick declined. They didn't want to go back there again.

As they left the police station, Leo and Nick knew they had to find out what was going on. They went to the library and started researching the area's history

"This is getting weirder by the minute," Nick said, looking around the room as if he expected something strange to happen.

Leo nodded in agreement, still feeling the sensation of the scratch on his back. He lay down on the bed and closed his eyes, trying to calm down. After a few minutes, he fell asleep.

He dreamed that he was in a forest, and someone was following him. He could hear footsteps behind him, but every time he turned around, there was no one there. Suddenly, he saw a figure standing in front of him, and it was the same young man he had seen near his window the night before. He had a sinister smile on his face.

"What do you want from me?" Leo asked.

"You know what I want," the young man said. "I want your soul."

Leo woke up screaming. Nick jumped up from the chair and rushed to Leo's side.

"Are you okay?" Nick asked, putting his hand on Leo's forehead.

"I had a nightmare," Leo said, still trembling.

Nick looked around the room, trying to find any signs of what could have caused Leo's nightmare, but everything seemed normal.

"We need to get out of here," Leo said, still feeling scared. "This place is not safe."

Nick nodded in agreement. They quickly packed their bags and left the room, not looking back.

As they were leaving the building, Leo noticed something strange. The building looked different from the outside. The windows were boarded up, and the door had a sign that read "condemned."

"What's going on?" Leo asked Nick.

"I don't know," Nick said, equally confused.

Leo and Nick couldn't believe it. They had stayed in a building with such a dark history. They wondered if the scratches and the nightmares were a result of the building's past.

They decided to leave the area and never come back. They knew they had experienced something they couldn't explain, and they didn't want to risk it happening again.

As they left the area, Leo and Nick couldn't shake off the feeling that they were being watched. They both looked back, but there was no one there. They got into their car and drove away, leaving the mysterious building behind.

II

The next few days, Leo and Nick tried to put their strange experience behind them. They continued their road trip, visiting new towns and cities, and taking in the sights and sounds of the places they visited. However, they couldn't shake off the feeling that something was off. They both felt like they were being followed, and the nightmares continued. One night, as they were setting up their tent in a deserted campground, Leo heard a strange noise. He got up to investigate, but couldn't find anything. As he was about to return to the tent, he heard a voice whisper his name.

"Leo," the voice said. "I'm still here."

Leo froze. He knew that voice. It was the same voice that had spoken to him in the condemned building. He turned around, but there was no one there.

"Nick!" he called out. "Did you hear that?"

"Hear what?" Nick replied, coming out of the tent.

"I heard a voice," Leo said, still looking around.

Nick looked at him skeptically. "Are you sure it wasn't just the wind?"

"I'm sure," Leo said, his voice trembling. "It was the same voice from the building."

Nick sighed. "Let's get some sleep. We have a long day tomorrow."

Leo nodded, but he couldn't shake off the feeling of unease. He knew that they were being followed, and he didn't know what to do.

The next day, Leo and Nick continued their road trip. They drove through beautiful landscapes and visited quaint towns, but they couldn't enjoy the scenery. They were both on edge, waiting for something to happen.

As they were driving down a deserted road, their car suddenly stalled. Nick tried to restart the engine, but it wouldn't budge.

"What's going on?" Leo asked.

"I don't know," Nick replied, trying to remain calm.

They both got out of the car and looked around. They were in the middle of nowhere, with no houses or buildings in sight.

"We need to find help," Leo said.

"Let's walk down the road and see if we can find a phone," Nick suggested.

They started walking down the road, hoping to find someone who could help them. After a few minutes, they saw a figure in the distance. As they got closer, they realized that it was a man.

"Excuse me," Leo said, approaching the man. "Our car broke down. Do you have a phone we can use?"

The man didn't say anything. He just stared at them with empty eyes.

"Is everything okay?" Nick asked.

The man suddenly lunged at them, his eyes turning red. Leo and Nick backed away, but the man was too fast. He grabbed Leo by the throat and lifted him off the ground.

"Leo!" Nick screamed, trying to pry the man's hands off.

Leo felt his air supply being cut off. He knew that he was going to die. Suddenly, he heard the same voice from the building.

"Leo," the voice said. "Give me your soul, and I'll let you go."

Leo didn't know what to do. He felt like he was being pulled in two directions. On one hand, he wanted to live. On the other hand, he didn't want to give up his soul.

Leo felt his consciousness slipping away. He knew that he was going to die if he didn't make a decision soon. He closed his eyes and tried to focus.

"Leo," the voice said again. "I'm waiting."

Leo opened his eyes and looked at the man who was strangling him. He saw something in the man's eyes that he hadn't seen before. Leo saw a glimmer of recognition in the man's eyes. It was as if he was fighting against the evil presence that had taken over his body.

"Fight it!" Leo shouted, using all the energy he had left.

The man suddenly shook his head and stumbled back, releasing Leo. Leo fell to the ground, gasping for air.

The man collapsed on the ground, his body writhing in pain. Leo and Nick watched in horror as his skin began to crack and peel away, revealing a dark, shadowy figure underneath.

The figure let out a deafening scream and disappeared into thin air.

Leo and Nick were both shaken to the core. They had just witnessed something truly terrifying.

"Let's get out of here," Nick said, helping Leo to his feet.

They ran back to their car, got in, and sped away as fast as they could.

Leo and Nick were both silent for the rest of the day. They were still processing what had happened on the road.

As they drove into the night, they saw a sign for a hotel and decided to stop for the night.

The hotel was a rundown place, but it was the only option in the area. They checked in and went to their room.

As they settled in, they heard strange noises coming from the hallway. It sounded like someone was walking around.

Leo got up to investigate. As he opened the door, he saw a shadowy figure disappear around the corner.

He followed it, but the figure was gone. He looked around, feeling a sense of unease.

"Leo, are you okay?" Nick asked, coming out of the room.

"I saw something," Leo replied. "I think we need to leave."

Leo and Nick packed up their things and left the hotel. They drove for hours, trying to put as much distance between themselves and the strange occurrences as possible.

As they drove, they saw a sign for a national park. Leo suggested that they stop and take a hike to clear their minds.

They parked the car and started walking. The scenery was breathtaking, and they both felt more relaxed than they had in days.

As they walked, they heard a rustling in the bushes. Leo went to investigate, but he found nothing.

Suddenly, he felt a sharp pain in his leg. He looked down and saw a snake slithering away.

"Leo, are you okay?" Nick asked, running over.

"I got bitten by a snake," Leo said, feeling dizzy.

They quickly got back to the car and drove to the nearest hospital.

Leo was treated for the snake bite and was given medication to ease the pain. As they left the hospital, they saw a sign for a nearby hot spring.

"Let's go relax in the hot spring," Nick suggested.

They followed the sign and found a secluded hot spring in the middle of the woods.

As they soaked in the warm water, they felt all their tension and stress melt away.

"This is just what we needed," Leo said, closing his eyes.

Suddenly, they heard a strange noise. They opened their eyes and saw a figure standing on the other side of the hot spring.

It was the same shadowy figure they had seen in the hotel.

Leo and Nick were frozen with fear. The figure stepped into the water and started walking towards them.

Leo and Nick both tried to get out of the hot spring, but they couldn't move.

The figure got closer and closer, and they could see that it was the same malevolent spirit they had encountered before.

"Leo, we have to banish it," Nick said, his voice shaking.

Leo nodded and closed his eyes. He focused his energy and started chanting the same.

Leo saw a glimmer of humanity in the man's eyes, and he knew what he had to do. He reached out and touched the man's hand, sending a surge of energy through him. The man let go of Leo and stumbled backward, his eyes returning to their normal color.

Leo gasped for breath and collapsed on the ground, feeling exhausted but relieved. Nick helped him up, and they both looked at the man who had attacked them. He was now standing a few feet away, looking dazed.

Leo and Nick walked over to him cautiously. They could see that he was struggling to remember what had happened.

"Are you okay?" Nick asked.

The man shook his head, looking confused. "I...I don't know what came over me."

"It's okay," Leo said, placing a hand on the man's shoulder. "We're just glad you're okay."

They walked back to their car, feeling shaken but grateful. They got in and started driving again, still trying to process what had just happened.

As they drove, Leo couldn't shake the feeling that they were being followed. He kept looking in the rearview mirror, but he couldn't see anything.

"Leo, do you feel that?" Nick asked suddenly.

Leo nodded. He could feel a chill in the air, and he knew that they were in danger.

"Step on it," Leo said, his voice urgent.

Nick pressed down on the gas pedal, and they sped down the road. But no matter how fast they went, they couldn't shake the feeling that something was coming for them.

Suddenly, they heard a loud bang, and their car swerved off the road. They crashed into a ditch, and the car rolled over several times before coming to a stop.

Leo and Nick were both hurt, but they managed to climb out of the car. As they stood there, looking at the wreckage, they saw a figure in the distance.

It was the same figure that had been following them all along. It was the malevolent spirit.

Leo and Nick knew that they had to fight for their lives. They stood their ground and faced the spirit, ready to do whatever it took to survive.

The spirit charged at them, but Leo and Nick were prepared. They used their newfound energy to create a shield around them, deflecting the spirit's attacks.

They fought for what felt like hours, but eventually, the spirit grew weaker. It let out a final scream and disappeared into the ether.

Leo and Nick collapsed on the ground, exhausted but victorious. They knew that they had faced their fears and come out on top.

As they lay there, looking up at the sky, they felt a sense of peace. They knew that they had done something important, and they knew that they would never forget the lessons they had learned on their road trip.

Leo and Nick eventually made it back home, but they were never the same. They had a newfound appreciation for life and for each other. They had faced their fears and come out on top, and they knew that they could face anything as long as they had each other.

Years later, as they sat by the campfire, they told their children and grandchildren the story of their road trip. They smiled as they remembered all the twists and turns they had faced, and they marveled at how far they had come.

And even though they were older now, and life had thrown many challenges their way, they knew that they could still conquer anything as long as they faced it together.

"Leo, Nick, over here!" a voice called out.

They turned around and saw a group of people running towards them. It was the group they had met earlier at the campground.

The group had heard the commotion and had come to investigate. They had brought weapons with them, ready to fight whatever was attacking Leo and Nick.

They charged at the man, hitting him with baseball bats and knives. The man fell to the ground, and his eyes returned to normal.

Leo gasped for air as Nick and the group helped him to his feet. They walked back to the cars and drove away, leaving the man and the strange phenomenon behind.

After they had driven for a few miles, they stopped at a gas station to call for help. Leo and Nick were both shaken by the experience, but they knew they had to keep going.

As they drove down the highway, they talked about what had happened. They wondered if they had just experienced a shared hallucination or if something truly supernatural was at work.

As the sun began to set, they reached their next destination – a small town nestled in the mountains. They decided to spend the night there, hoping to find some peace and quiet.

They checked into a cozy bed and breakfast and explored the town. They walked around the quaint shops and restaurants, trying to forget about the strange events of the past few days.

But as they walked, they felt like they were being watched. They heard strange whispers in their ears and saw shadows move in the corners of their vision.

Leo and Nick tried to ignore it, but they knew that something was wrong. They returned to the bed and breakfast and tried to get some rest, hoping that they would feel better in the morning.

But as they lay in their beds, they heard strange noises in the hallway. They heard footsteps that didn't belong to anyone in the bed and breakfast.

They got out of bed and cautiously opened the door. They saw a shadowy figure moving down the hallway. They tried to follow it, but it disappeared into thin air.

Leo and Nick knew that they had to find out what was going on. They decided to investigate the town the next day, hoping to find answers.

The next morning, they walked around the town, asking questions and searching for clues. They learned that the town had a dark history, filled with tales of witchcraft and supernatural occurrences.

They visited a local library and read books on the town's history. They learned that the town was built on the site of an ancient Native American burial ground. Many of the town's residents believed that the spirits of the dead still haunted the town to this day.

Leo and Nick knew that they had to do something to put the spirits to rest. They talked to the town's residents and learned that there was an abandoned mine outside of town. The mine was said to be a gateway to the spirit world.

Leo and Nick decided to investigate the mine. They knew that it was dangerous, but they had to do something to put the spirits to rest.

As they made their way into the mine, they heard strange noises and felt a chill in the air. They saw shadows moving in the darkness and heard whispers in their ears.

They pushed forward, determined to find the source of the paranormal activity. As they turned a corner, they saw a figure standing in the distance.

It was the same figure that had haunted them since the beginning of their trip. The figure turned around and revealed itself to be a woman.

The woman had pale skin and black hair. Her eyes were dark and sunken, and she wore a tattered dress.

The woman started to walk towards them, and Leo and Nick could feel her energy getting stronger.

They closed their eyes and focused their energy.

They chanted a few words that the psychic had given them, hoping to banish the spirit.

As they chanted, they felt a powerful force pushing back against them. They knew that they had to keep going, so they continued to chant.

Finally, the force broke, and the woman disappeared. Leo and Nick opened their eyes and saw that the mine was now silent.

As they emerged from the mine, they saw that the townspeople had gathered around the entrance. They were all looking at them with a mix of awe and fear. Leo and Nick felt like they had just been through a nightmare, and they didn't know how to explain what had just happened.

The psychic appeared beside them, smiling. "You did it!" she exclaimed. "You broke the curse!"

Leo and Nick thanked the psychic for her help and asked her how she knew about the curse. She explained that she had sensed the witch's presence and had been searching for someone brave enough to break the curse.

The townspeople approached them, thanking them for their bravery. Leo and Nick were relieved that the curse had been broken, but they couldn't shake off the feeling that something wasn't right. They had a sense that there was more to the story than what they had just experienced.

As they walked back to their car, they noticed that the townspeople were watching them intently. It was as if they were waiting for something to happen.

Suddenly, a piercing scream echoed through the town. Leo and Nick ran towards the source of the sound and found the psychic lying on the ground, surrounded by a group of shadowy figures.

The figures were the same as the ones they had seen in the mine, and they were holding the psychic captive. Leo and Nick knew that they had to act fast to save her.

They charged at the figures, ready to fight. But as they got closer, they realized that they were no match for the creatures. The figures were too powerful, and their dark energy was overwhelming.

Leo and Nick were captured, just like the psychic. They were taken to a dark underground lair, where they found themselves face to face with the source of the paranormal activity – the witch.

The witch had somehow survived their attempt to break the curse, and she was now more powerful than ever. She revealed to them that she had been using the mine as a portal to the underworld, and that she had been summoning the shadowy figures to do her bidding.

Leo and Nick were horrified by the witch's revelation. They knew that they had to stop her before it was too late.

But how? They were trapped in the witch's lair, with no way out.

Suddenly, they remembered the words that the psychic had given them. They closed their eyes and focused their energy, chanting the words with all their might.

The witch laughed at them, mocking their feeble attempts to stop her. But as they continued to chant, they felt a surge of power coursing through their bodies.

The ground shook beneath them, and the walls of the lair started to crumble. The witch's power was weakening, and she knew that she was in trouble.

Leo and Nick seized the opportunity to break free from their restraints. They charged at the witch, determined to put an end to her reign of terror.

The witch fought back, using all her dark magic to try and defeat them. But Leo and Nick were not afraid. They knew that they had the power of the psychic's words on their side.

The battle raged on, with neither side gaining the upper hand. But just when it seemed like all was lost, the ground shook once more, and a blinding light filled the lair.

When the light dissipated, Leo and Nick found themselves back in the sunlight. The town was in ruins, but they were alive.

They looked at each other, unsure of what had just happened. Had they won the battle? Had they defeated the witch?

Suddenly, they heard a voice behind them. It was the psychic, alive and well. She explained that they had been transported back in time, to before the witch had cursed the mine.

The psychic revealed that the curse had never been broken, and that the witch was still out there, waiting for someone to break the curse and free her from her prison.

Leo and Nick knew that they had to try again. They had to break the curse once and for all, and put an end to the witch's reign of terror.

And so, they set out on a new journey, to find a way to break the curse and defeat the witch. They knew that the road ahead was long and dangerous, but they were determined to succeed. They searched far and wide for answers, seeking out ancient texts and consulting with other psychics and experts in the paranormal.

As they delved deeper into the mystery, they discovered that the curse was even more complex than they had thought. It involved ancient rituals and sacrifices, and they would need to uncover the truth and understand the witch's motives in order to break it.

The journey was grueling, and they faced countless obstacles along the way. They were attacked by shadowy figures and almost lost their lives in the process.

But they persisted, driven by a sense of duty and a desire to put an end to the witch's evil. They were getting closer to the truth, and they could feel that the end was near.

Finally, after months of searching, they found what they were looking for. A dusty tome hidden in a forgotten corner of a library revealed the final piece of the puzzle.

They knew what they had to do. They prepared themselves for the final battle, gathering all the knowledge and tools they had acquired along the way.

As they approached the mine once again, they felt a sense of dread wash over them. They knew that this was it – the final showdown.

They entered the mine cautiously, their senses on high alert. They could feel the witch's presence around them, and they knew that she was watching their every move.

As they made their way through the tunnels, they encountered more and more shadowy figures, each one more terrifying than the last.

But they did not falter. They had come too far to give up now.

Finally, they reached the cavern with the small lake and the island. And there she was, the witch, waiting for them.

The witch laughed at them, confident in her power. But Leo and Nick were not intimidated. They knew that they had the knowledge and the tools to defeat her.

They recited the words from the ancient tome, and the witch's power started to weaken. She let out a bloodcurdling scream, and the ground shook beneath them.

The witch fought back with all her might, but it was no use. Leo and Nick were too strong.

And then, just as they were about to deliver the final blow, something unexpected happened. The witch's eyes widened in shock, and she let out a gasp.

"No," she whispered. "It can't be."

And then, with a blinding flash of light, the witch disappeared into thin air.

Leo and Nick were stunned. They had won. They had defeated the witch and broken the curse.

But as they made their way back to the surface, they couldn't shake off the feeling that something was off. They could feel eyes on them, watching their every move.

And then they heard a voice, a voice that they recognized all too well. It was the voice of the witch, and she was laughing.

Leo and Nick froze in terror. They had defeated the witch, but had they truly broken the curse? Or had they just unleashed something even more terrifying?

The ground shook once more, and the entrance to the mine was blocked once again. Leo and Nick were trapped.

They looked at each other, their hearts pounding with fear. They knew that they were in for another long, grueling journey. But they were ready. They had defeated the witch once, and they would do it again, no matter the cost.

And so, they set out on a new journey, more determined than ever to put an end to the witch. The journey was different this time. It was darker, more treacherous. They were no longer seeking answers but trying to escape the witch's wrath.

The shadowy figures that they had encountered before were back, and this time they were more aggressive. They could feel the witch's power growing stronger, and they knew that they were running out of time.

As they made their way through the labyrinthine tunnels, they could hear the witch's laughter echoing through the darkness.

And then, just when they thought that they were getting closer to the surface, they encountered something that stopped them in their tracks. It was a door, a door that they had never seen before.

They could feel the witch's power emanating from the door, and they knew that they had to get through it if they were to escape.

They tried to open the door, but it wouldn't budge. They tried everything they could think of, but nothing worked.

And then, just when they were about to give up, they heard a faint whisper. It was a voice that they didn't recognize, and it was coming from the other side of the door.

They listened carefully, and the voice grew louder. It was the voice of a young girl, and she was crying.

Leo and Nick exchanged a look. They knew that they had to help the girl, no matter what.

They focused their energy and chanted the words that they had learned from the ancient tome. The door shook, and then it slowly creaked open.

As they stepped through the door, they found themselves in a small room. There was a girl there, just as they had heard. She was huddled in a corner, her eyes wide with fear.

Leo and Nick approached her cautiously, trying to reassure her that they were there to help.

And then, just as they were about to reach her, something unexpected happened. The girl disappeared into thin air.

Leo and Nick looked at each other, stunned. What was going on? Had the witch done this?

And then they heard a voice, a voice that they recognized all too well. It was the voice of the witch, and she was laughing.

"You fools," she cackled. "You thought you could defeat me? You thought you could break my curse? You were wrong. You were all wrong."

The ground shook, and the walls of the room started to close in on them. Leo and Nick knew that they had to get out, and fast.

They ran towards the door, but it wouldn't budge. They were trapped.

And then, just as they were about to give up, something unexpected happened. A beam of light shone down from above, illuminating the room.

Leo and Nick looked up, and they saw something that they had never seen before. It was a portal, a portal to another world.

They knew that they had no other choice. They had to go through the portal if they were to escape the witch's wrath.

They stepped through the portal, and they found themselves in a world unlike any other. It was a world of darkness and shadows, a world where anything could happen.

And then, just as they were getting used to their new surroundings, they heard a sound. It was a sound that they had heard before. It was the sound of the witch's laughter.

Leo and Nick looked at each other, their hearts pounding with fear. They knew that they were in for a long, grueling journey. But they were ready. They had defeated the witch before, and they knew that they could do it again. They steeled themselves for what was to come and began to move forward. As they walked through the dark and foreboding world, they could feel the witch's presence getting stronger. Her laughter grew louder, and they knew that they were getting closer. Suddenly, the ground began to shake, and the sky turned red. Leo and Nick knew that they had reached the witch's lair. They cautiously made their way towards the source of the disturbance, and as they drew closer, they could see the witch standing before them, her eyes blazing with an otherworldly fire. The witch let out a chilling cackle and raised her hands. Leo and Nick knew that they had to act fast, or they would be doomed. They focused their energy and chanted the words that they had learned from the ancient tome. The witch's power began to wane, and her eyes widened in fear. "No!" she screamed. "You cannot defeat me!" But it was too late. Leo and Nick had broken her curse and were now free from her grasp. The witch let out a final scream and disappeared into thin air. Leo and Nick breathed a sigh of relief. They had done it. They had defeated the witch and saved themselves from a terrible fate. They turned to leave, but then something caught their eye.

It was a book, lying on the ground where the witch had stood. Leo picked up the book and examined it closely. It was an old and tattered tome, bound in leather and marked with strange symbols. Leo and Nick looked at each other, a sense of foreboding washing over them. They knew that the book was powerful, and they knew that they had to be careful. They decided to take the book with them, but they knew that they had to keep it hidden. They couldn't let the power of the book fall into the wrong hands. As they made their way back to the portal, Leo and Nick could feel the weight of the book in their backpack. They knew that their journey wasn't over yet, and they knew that they had to be vigilant. And then, just as they were about to step through the portal, they heard a sound. It was the sound of footsteps, echoing through the darkness. Leo and Nick turned to face the source of the sound, their hearts pounding with fear. They knew that they were not alone. Someone, or something, was following them. They stepped through the portal, hoping that they had left their pursuer behind. But as they emerged on the other side, they knew that they were wrong. Standing before them, blocking their path, was a figure cloaked in shadow. They couldn't see its face, but they could feel its malevolent energy. Leo and Nick took a step back, unsure of what to do. They had defeated the witch, but they knew that they were no match for whatever this thing was. And then, just as they were about to turn and run, the figure spoke. Its voice was cold and mocking, and it sent shivers down their spines. "You thought that you had won," it said. "But you were wrong. The power of the book is too great for you to handle. You should have left it where it was." Leo and Nick exchanged a look, a sense of dread settling over them. They knew that they were in trouble. And then the figure stepped forward, and Leo and Nick were plunged into darkness. The last thing they heard was the sound of the figure's laughter,

Printed by Libri Plureos GmbH in Hamburg,
Germany